Dedication

This book is dedicated to my youngest Franklin Edison, his vivacious spirit is the sountrack of my heartbeat.

Written By P.E. Barnes
&
Illustrated By Aria Jones

This is Franklin; he is the owner of a chain of franchise restaurants.

Franklin started as a teenager working as a cashier at a fast-food restaurant to save for a car. While working, Franklin developed a passion for service and witnessed the profitability of the business.

Franklin went to college to study accounting and graduated with a bachelor's degree. He returned back to his community and worked at the restaurant as a manager and learned the business.

Franklin saved his earnings from his job and used the funds to invest in buying a franchise. All those years of hard work paid off, and he was now the proud owner of a McDonald's.

He employed many people from his community to help run the restaurant. He also mentored other young people that expressed interest in owning their own franchise.

Franklin met a beautiful woman, Mya, while working in his business.

A Franchise owner is someone who buys a business that is part of a chain business. The franchise owner uses the formula, logo, name, and model of an established chain business. This business model can be very successful and lead to wealth.

Mya was an attorney, and they fell in love, got married, and had four children.

Franklin went on to acquire nearly 20 more franchises before his retirement. His children now enjoy running the restaurants.

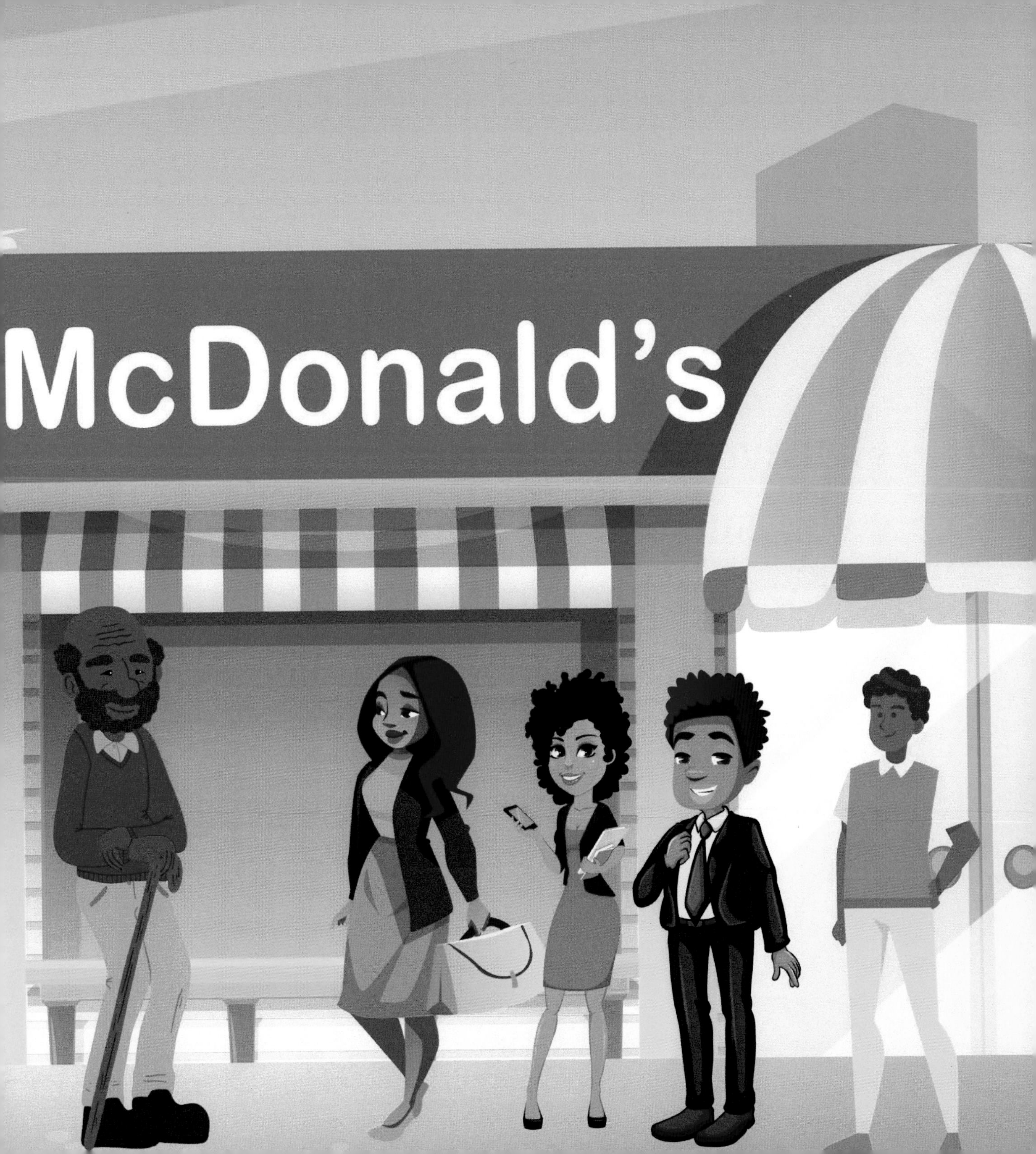
McDonald's

Franklin is very well respected by his community and his family. He has a rich legacy of giving others employment opportunities and leaving his children a great inheritance.

Vocabulary Words

Inheritance – *anything such as property, businesses, money, jewelry, etc., handed down from the past, from an ancestor or predecessor.*

Legacy – *leaving behind a glorious past; or a gift by will of money or other personal property.*

Franchise – *a business model that allows you (the franchisee) to start your business by legally using someone else's (the franchisor) expertise, ideas, and processes.*

Profitability – *yielding profit or financial gain.*

Profit – *a financial gain; the difference between the amount earned and the amount spent in buying, operating, or producing something.*

Mentor – *someone more experienced or knowledgeable helps to guide a less experienced person.*

Celebrity Franchise Owners

1. Shaquille O'Neal – owns over 100 "Five Guys" restaurants.
2. Rick Ross – owns several "Wingstop" restaurants.
3. Chris Brown – owns 14 "Burger King" restaurants.
4. Magic Johnson – owns more than 25 "Burger King" restaurants.
5. Venus Williams – owns several "Jamba Juice" franchises.

My Franchise Goals

The End

24

About the Author

P.E. Barnes is a real estate investor in Chicago. She is passionate about educating children about financial literacy. She is a wife and mother of two young boys that inspired this book series.

For bookings or inquiries email: littleowners@gmail.com

Made in the USA
Monee, IL
06 November 2020